ANIMAL ARK

Fox Cub Danger

Fox Cub Danger

Lucy Daniels

With special thanks to Lucy Courtenay

ORCHARD BOOKS

First published in Great Britain in 2018 by The Watts Publishing Group

1 3 5 7 9 10 8 6 4 2

Text copyright © Working Partners Ltd, 2018
Illustrations copyright © Working Partners Ltd, 2018

A CIP catalogue record for this book
is available from the British Library.

ISBN 978 1 40835 402 5

Printed and bound in Great Britain by CPI Group (UK) Ltd, Croydon, CR0 4YY

The paper and board used in this book are made from wood from responsible sources.

Orchard Books
An imprint of
Hachette Children's Group
Part of The Watts Publishing Group Limited
Carmelite House
50 Victoria Embankment
London EC4Y 0DZ

An Hachette UK Company
www.hachette.co.uk
www.hachettechildrens.co.uk

CONTENTS

CHAPTER ONE

The ginger kitten clambered under
Amelia's jumper, popped up through her
collar and batted at her long blonde hair.

"I think he likes me!" Amelia said,
pulling the kitten out of her jumper.

Her friend Sam grinned at her. He
was stroking one of the kitten's three

tortoiseshell sisters, while the other two
scampered around the tiled floor of the
Animal Ark veterinary surgery. Their
mum, Caramel, was curled up asleep on
a cushion in the far corner.

Sam's kitten scrambled up his arm
and perched on his head. "Hey!" he said
with a smile, peeling her off. "I'm not a
cat basket!"

He put her back on the floor, and Amelia lifted the ginger kitten down too.

Flicking their little tails and twitching their ears, the four kittens pounced and rolled and chased each other, skidding on the tiles. When Amelia and Sam had found them they had just been newborns, with their ears folded close to their heads and their eyes tightly closed. Now, a month on, their green eyes were wide and unblinking, their whiskers quivering and their ears pricked and alert.

"It's great that we've got homes for two of them already," Amelia said, watching the kittens batting at each other with their little paws.

"Just two more to go," said Sam.

Amelia and Sam were determined to find new homes for all four kittens, once they were old enough to leave their mum. Amelia hoped it would show Mr and Mrs Hope, the vets who owned the surgery, that they were responsible enough to help out at Animal Ark all the time. She couldn't imagine anything more wonderful than spending every day surrounded by animals!

Amelia wished she could adopt a kitten herself, but she and her mum had only just moved in with her gran in Welford, and she was still getting used to her new life. Besides, every other weekend she

visited her dad back in York, so having
a pet might be tricky. *I'll just have to
play with these kittens as much as I can*, she
thought.

A red-haired lady in a
white vet's coat put her
head round the door.

"It's great to see how
confident the kittens are
becoming," remarked
Mrs Hope. "You're
doing brilliantly!"

"We love them," said
Amelia at once. She
flushed with pride –
playing with the kittens

wasn't just fun, it was doing an important job of getting them used to being around people, so they would become happy pets. "Honestly, Mrs Hope, we could play with the kittens all day."

Mrs Hope laughed, her nose crinkling. "Well, thank you both," she said. "It's *very* helpful!"

Amelia exchanged a pleased look with Sam. He glanced at the clock on the wall. "Oops, it's eleven!" he said, scrambling to his feet. "Mum and Dad said I had to tidy the guest lounge this morning. Mac, er, untidied it." Mac was Sam's puppy – he was adorable but naughty, and always causing trouble at the bed and breakfast run by Sam's parents.

"I'll come and help," Amelia offered.

They settled the cat family back into their pen, where the kittens nuzzled into Caramel's soft fur. Then they headed back into reception. Julia Kaminski, the receptionist, was pinning a poster to the Animal Ark noticeboard.

ANIMAL PHOTOGRAPHY EXHIBITION!

GORGEOUS GUINEA PIG?
HANDSOME HAWK?
CUTE COW?
ENTER YOUR ANIMAL PHOTOGRAPHS AND YOU COULD WIN A PRIZE!

"It was Mr Hope's idea," Julia explained, propelling her wheelchair back over to the reception desk. "It'll be fun for everyone to see the amazing animals we have in Welford."

Amelia turned excitedly to Sam. "We should take a photo of Mac and enter the competition!"

"If he stays still long enough," Sam joked. "Come on. Mum and Dad will wonder where I am."

CHAPTER TWO

They set off towards the Old Mill B&B. Amelia still wasn't used to living in Welford. In York, everything smelled of bus fumes and wet pavements. Welford had a greener, fresher sort of smell. And there were animals *everywhere* – ducks on the pond, doves balancing

on a telephone wire overhead, a cat
watching them lazily from a fence post.
Amelia wished she had a camera with
her right now!

Sam opened the Old Mill's front door.
They went into the hall, which had a
reception desk and a display of leaflets
advertising tourist attractions. Mac
came bounding over to meet them,

wagging his tail
and panting with
excitement. Amelia
kneeled down on
the floor to pat
his scruffy
white fur.

"Hi, Mac!" Amelia said. "It's good to see you, too!" Then from one of the rooms came the sound of raised voices. Amelia exchanged a startled look with Sam. "What's going on?"

Sam frowned. "I don't know. But it's coming from the guest lounge."

Sam darted down a corridor and Amelia followed, with Mac's claws scrabbling on the floorboards as he scurried to keep up. Sam stopped, held a finger to his lips, then stepped through into the guest lounge. Amelia followed him into the room. It had sunny yellow walls, a thick, fluffy white rug and a long cream sofa. But there were cushions, books and ornaments scattered all over the floor, and furniture pushed into the middle of the room.

"Wow," muttered Sam. "It's even messier than when I left it."

Mr Baxter was on his hands and knees, peering underneath the sofa. All they could see of Mrs Baxter was her outline behind the long cream curtains.

"Hi, Mum and Dad," said Sam. "Er … have you lost something?"

"Mr Ferguson's motorbike gloves," said Mrs Baxter, stepping out from behind the curtains. She usually looked very smart, but today her hair was a mess, her shirt was crumpled and her brow was furrowed with worry. "Oh, hello, dear," she said, noticing Amelia. "His gloves were hanging on the washing line this morning, but they've disappeared."

"Because that puppy took them!" roared a voice.

Amelia jumped. Mr Ferguson, one of the B&B's regular guests, was standing behind her, an angry glare on his bearded face. He made Amelia think of a grizzly bear who had woken up from hibernation too early.

"That pup is capable of anything," Mr Ferguson growled. "If you don't find my gloves, I'll never stay at this B&B again!" He stomped off. Amelia could hear his heavy tread as he went up the stairs to his room.

"Mac didn't do it," said Sam, crossing his arms.

Mr Baxter got to his feet. "It wouldn't be the first time Mac has taken something that doesn't belong to him, would it? Remember when he chewed up my toothbrush?"

"But Mac wouldn't have taken the gloves," Sam protested. "Anyway, he's too small to reach the washing line."

Mrs Baxter put an arm round Sam's shoulders. "We can't keep Mac if he drives away our guests, Sam," she said gently. "He's a lovely puppy, but he's more trouble than we ever thought he'd be. I'm so sorry, love, but if this continues we might have to find him a new home."

Amelia's heart ached at the distraught look on Sam's face. He wrenched away from his mother, scooped up Mac and ran from the room.

Amelia followed him out into the garden. She found him sitting on a bench, rubbing his face with his sleeve. Mac seemed to know Sam was upset, and lay at his feet, his head on his paws and his ears drooping.

Amelia sat next to him. "It'll be all right," she said. "We can teach Mac not to take things. We've taught him loads already, haven't we? He doesn't chew things any more, and he hasn't weed indoors for ages."

Sam nodded, and his face brightened a little.

"Let's take him for a walk now," Amelia suggested. "We can practise a few commands. What do you think?"

"That's a good idea," said Sam. "Thanks, Amelia." He ran indoors to fetch Mac's lead and clipped it on to the puppy's collar. "Heel, Mac," he said.

Mac trotted nicely beside Sam, close to his heels, as they walked back up the drive. They headed towards a dark fringe of woodland that ran alongside the road, then they turned down a path. It was cool among the trees and the leaves rustled peacefully.

"He's doing well, isn't he?" said Sam, looking down proudly at Mac as he walked beside them.

There was a burst of song above them, and a robin flittered down to the path, bright scarlet feathers on its chest.

"Hi!" said Sam. Turning to Amelia, he explained, "I see him almost every day when I take Mac out. You get to know the woods well if you keep your eyes open." He pointed to a series of dusty dips and holes in a clearing through the trees. "You see those? It's a badger sett."

"Wow!" said Amelia. "You know loads about wildlife. Do you think we'll see some badgers?"

Sam grinned and shook his head. "Looks like they abandoned that sett ages ago."

The robin chirped and flew off. Mac yapped at the flash of feathers – then took off at a sprint through the trees, yanking the lead from Sam's hand.

"Mac!" cried Sam in alarm. He clapped his hands to his head. "Oh no, he was doing so well!"

"Come back, Mac!" Amelia called.

They chased after the puppy, leaping over the branches and bracken that lay

across the path. Up ahead, Amelia saw
a tall boy in jeans and a green hoodie,
peering through a camera with a huge
lens – and Mac was running straight
towards his legs.

He's going to smash right into him!
Amelia thought with panic.

"Watch out!" she shouted.

The boy lowered his camera. He started when he saw Mac, then put the camera aside just in time and caught the puppy around his furry, white tummy.

"Hey!" he laughed. "What's the rush?"

Ecstatic at the attention, Mac licked the boy's face all over. Amelia recognised him now. It was Josh Cleary, an older boy from school. He had hazel eyes and more freckles than Amelia had ever seen. The colour of his hair made her think of the ginger kitten.

"Sorry, Josh," said Sam, gasping for breath as he grabbed Mac's lead. "I hope he didn't spoil your photo."

Josh rubbed Mac's ears. "Don't worry.

I was trying to take a picture of a deer, but it had already run away." He turned to Amelia. "Hi," he said. "Don't I know you from school?"

"I'm in Sam's class," Amelia said. "I've only just started, though. You're in the year above, aren't you?"

Josh nodded. "Are you walking back into the village? I'll come with you."

As they walked, Josh swiped through the other photos he'd taken that day. When he showed them a particularly good picture of a woodpecker on a branch, its head cocked to one side, Amelia remembered something.

"Have you heard about the animal

photo competition at Animal Ark?" she asked him.

Josh's eyes lit up. "No, but that sounds really cool. Maybe I'll enter!"

They came out of the wood, and they were just passing Welford's little supermarket when Mac began straining towards a red car parked outside.

"Stop it, Mac!" said Sam, panting with the effort of keeping him under control.

"Why's he so interested in that car?" wondered Amelia.

"There isn't even anyone inside it," Josh pointed out.

Amelia hurried over to the car. She kneeled down, peered underneath it –

and gasped. Beside one of the wheels
was an orange-furred creature with a
pointed snout and a long, fluffy tail.

"It's a fox!" she said.

CHAPTER THREE

The fox's wild eyes flashed at Amelia.
Its face was nearly as delicate as a
cat's, though it was a little bigger. As it
flattened its black-tipped ears against its
head, Amelia noticed that one of them
was wet with blood.

"He's hurt!" she gasped.

Sam and Josh kneeled down beside Amelia to look.

"Oh, wow," breathed Josh.

The fox snarled at them, showing its pointed teeth. They quickly drew back, not wanting to scare the injured animal.

Mac whined and hid behind Sam's legs.

"I think it must be really hurt," said Amelia. "Otherwise it would

run away from us, wouldn't it?" She
eyed the road, and the woods on the
other side. What could have happened?

She crouched down to take another
look. The fox was panting and it snarled
again. Amelia desperately wanted to
take care of it, but she was sure it would
bite if she got any closer.

"We can't leave it here," said Sam.

"Mr and Mrs Hope will know what
to do," Amelia said. "Let's call Animal
Ark."

While Josh, Sam and Mac went inside
the supermarket to use the phone,
Amelia stayed with the fox. Its wild
orange eyes watched her fearfully.

"You're safe now," she said, as gently as she could. "We're going to help you."

The fox just watched her silently, its whiskers quivering.

🐾 🐾 🐾 🐾

After a short wait, the Hopes picked up the fox in their van, gave it a sedative to make it sleep, then drove them all to Animal Ark.

"Well done for finding him," said Mrs Hope, as Mr Hope took the fox off for an X-ray.

"I think his leg is broken," said Mrs Hope, leading Amelia, Sam and Josh back to reception. "He would have been in big trouble if you hadn't called us when you did."

"It was Mac who found him really," said Sam proudly. "He's a hero."

"Yes, he is," said Mrs Hope, patting the puppy. "It shouldn't take too long for a result. If you wait here, I'll let you know when the X-ray is ready."

They sat down on the comfy chairs in reception. Amelia nudged Josh, pointing out the poster about the photography competition.

Josh looked thoughtful. "I bet there'll be loads of entries," he said. "I'll have to take a really amazing photo – but of what?"

Amelia jumped up. "The kittens!" She turned to the receptionist. "Julia, is it OK if we go and see Caramel and her kittens?"

"Of course," said Julia, who was typing at the computer on her desk. "I'll watch Mac while you're gone."

Sam looped Mac's lead over a hook on the wall, and he and Amelia led Josh to

the room where the kittens were staying.
New patients had arrived since earlier
that morning: a tortoise with a splint,
and a sleepy dog with a plastic collar
around her neck to stop her from licking
the stitches in her leg.

Sam opened Caramel's cage. The
four kittens blinked up at them. Amelia
lifted out the ginger one and passed him
carefully to Josh.

"They're so cute! And this one matches my hair," Josh said with a grin. "What are their names?

"Their mum's called Caramel," said Sam. "Mr Stevens the farmer is adopting her and the tortoiseshell kitten with the white tip on her tail. She's called Snowdrop."

"Mrs Cranbourne's adopting that one," said Amelia, pointing to the liveliest tortoiseshell, who was chasing her tail. "Her name's Miss Fizz."

"We still need to find homes for the ginger one and the last tortoiseshell," Sam said.

"We haven't named them," explained Amelia. "We think it will be harder to say goodbye to them if we do that."

That didn't mean Amelia didn't have a hundred names in her head, of course. Marmalade and Apricot were at the top of her list for the ginger one, and she liked Star for the tortoiseshell because of the white patch above one eye, shaped just like a five-pointed star. Star's eyes twinkled, and Amelia bent down to smooth the kitten's little head.

Josh passed the ginger kitten to Amelia and switched on his camera. But when he took a photo, the flash went off with a bright flare of light and the tortoiseshell kittens darted off to take cover under a chair.

"Sorry, kittens," said Josh apologetically, as Sam crawled under the chair to coax the kittens out. "I'll turn the flash off."

"I think this one actually liked it!" said Amelia, stroking the ginger kitten. It was struggling to get out of her hands and rush towards the camera. Josh held the camera closer, and the kitten batted at it playfully.

Meanwhile, the tortoiseshells were scrambling over Sam like he was a climbing frame. Josh stood on a chair to get an overhead view as they scampered and played, his camera clicking as he took shot after shot.

When he'd finished, Amelia and Sam looked over his shoulder as he swiped through the pictures. Every single shot was blurry! "I don't think I'll win anything with these," Josh said, but he was grinning anyway. "Those kittens are so funny!"

"What's the best picture you've ever taken?" Amelia asked.

Josh looked shy. "I took a few last week that I'm quite pleased with." He skipped through to them. Amelia and Sam gazed, impressed, at shots of an owl swooping through black branches, a mouse scurrying through some leaves and a prowling fox with glowing eyes.

Amelia wondered if it was the fox they had rescued, but decided that its tail was too light.

"How did you get so close to them?" she asked.

"My mum's a photographer," Josh explained. "She helped me build a hide so I can watch the animals without disturbing them."

"What's a hide?" Sam asked.

"It's like a shelter," Josh explained. "The animals can't see you inside it, but you can see them."

Mr Hope put his head round the door. "The X-rays are finished," he said.

They put the kittens back in the

pen with Caramel, then went into the
consulting room with the two vets.

The fox was recovering in a pen, stirring
sleepily on its heat pad. It had a bandage
tied carefully across its hurt ear now.
Amelia admired the red and orange
shades of its thick coat before turning
her attention to the X-ray images on
the computer screen.

"These are the leg bones," said Mr Hope, pointing to the white shapes in the pictures. "We were worried they were fractured, but luckily they're not."

"He's badly bruised and scratched, though," Mrs Hope added. "His ear was hurt, and his claws are torn, so we think that he was hit by a car and dragged along the road."

"Poor fox," said Sam.

"He'll make a good recovery," said Mrs Hope. "And then we can release him back into the wild."

"The trouble is," Mr Hope added, "we can't release him where you found him. He could get hit by another car."

"If only we knew where his den was," sighed Mrs Hope. "He'd be safe there."

Even though she had no idea what a fox's den looked like, Amelia felt a swell of determination in her chest. She glanced at Sam, and the firm set of his jaw told her he was thinking the same thing. This was another chance to prove to the Hopes how useful they could be at Animal Ark.

"We'll find his den," promised Amelia. *Even if we have to search every leaf of the woods, we'll find the fox's home!*

CHAPTER FOUR

"Sam!" Amelia said, as they stood in the Welford supermarket car park the next day. "You're not listening to what I'm saying!"

"I am, honestly," Sam said over his shoulder. Mac was zigzagging around the empty car park with his nose pressed to the ground. "It's just Mac's really excited about being here again."

Amelia had stayed up late, researching foxes on her tablet. Her dreams had been full of foxes and badgers and kittens and dark, twisty woods. She started telling Sam what she'd found out as he fought to keep his balance – Mac was pulling him in all directions.

"Fox dens are called earths," she said. "They're often underground, but not always. The holes are usually wider than they are tall, and there's always lots of dug earth outside."

"Earths, check," Sam panted. "Underground, check. Did you read anything about pavements? Mac is really interested in this one."

Mac was snuffling at a small patch of concrete, where the car park met the road. Dandelions sprouted out of a crack in it. Amelia crouched down and studied the small, dark patches beside the weeds. Her nose wrinkled.

"I think this is blood," she said cautiously. Sam's eyes widened.

The car the fox had been hiding under was now gone. Amelia and Sam moved around the empty parking spaces, looking for clumps of fur, more drops of blood – anything.

Mac wagged his tail at everyone who walked past.

After a few minutes, Sam pointed at the road. "What about those marks?" he asked. "Do you think they're important?"

Amelia squinted at the black squiggles. They veered from one lane into another, then back again. "They look like … tyre marks," she said. "Like a car was swerving around something."

"Something like a fox," said Sam slowly.

Amelia nodded. "It all fits, doesn't it? Blood and tyre marks … Mr and Mrs Hope thought the fox had been hit by a car. Maybe if we find more clues, they will lead us back to its den."

At the side of the road, Mac was straining so hard on his lead that he was almost standing up on his hind legs.

"Mac's got a scent," said Sam eagerly. "It could be another clue!"

"Good boy, Mac," said Amelia. "Come on, show us what your nose is telling you!"

His tail wagging furiously, Mac led them across the road – Amelia and Sam carefully checking for traffic first – and into the wood on the other side, along a narrow path through brambles and bracken. Then he suddenly hurtled off the path, yanking his lead from Sam's hand,

and through a patch of ferns, barking.

"He's found something!" Sam shouted.

The den! Amelia thought, hope surging within her. They rushed after Mac, jumping over fallen branches and dodging prickly brambles.

Mac stopped, tail wagging. Amelia felt like a balloon deflating when she saw what he was sniffing at – a pile of animal droppings at the base of a large oak tree. Mac threw himself on to the ground and squirmed around in the smelly mess, his legs in the air.

"Oh, Mac!" Sam groaned. "You're supposed to find the fox den, not a pile of poo!"

Amelia held her nose. "That's so gross," she said, though she couldn't help laughing at the ridiculous sight.

Sam hauled Mac out of the droppings. The little Westie's white coat was now covered in blackish-green streaks, but his tail was wagging delightedly.

"Hey," said Amelia, "I was reading about dog training as well as foxes last night. When dogs pull on their leads too much, you're supposed to cut their walk short."

"OK," said Sam. "We need to give him a bath now anyway."

There was the sound of running feet on the path behind them. Amelia turned to see her neighbour, Dr Kent, jogging their way, wearing grey shorts, a T-shirt and blue running shoes. Amelia often saw him running around Welford in the mornings.

"Oh dear, what a mess," Dr Kent said, stopping and taking out his headphones. "Fox droppings, eh? My dog Monty likes rolling in those."

Amelia and Sam glanced at each other.

"Fox droppings?" said Amelia.

"Yes," said Dr Kent. "Their smell is so … er … unique, that they're easy to recognise. Dogs used to roll in fox droppings to disguise their own scent when they were hunting, and they still like doing it now."

"We're looking for a fox den, Dr Kent," explained Amelia, hope rising inside her again. "Have you seen one anywhere around here?"

Dr Kent shook his head. "Afraid not. But I often see a pair of foxes during my runs through the woods." He put his headphones back in. "Good luck with your search."

"A pair of foxes," repeated Amelia, when Dr Kent had vanished through the bracken. She looked at Sam. "If there's a *pair* of foxes ..."

"Then the injured fox must have a mate somewhere!" said Sam eagerly.

"Exactly." Amelia grinned. "And if we can find his mate, she'll hopefully lead us to the den!"

"We're getting closer," said Sam. "But we've really got to get the poo off Mac first. I don't think I can stand the smell much longer."

Back at the B&B, Amelia unwound the garden hose and Sam turned on the tap. Water spurted out, and Amelia aimed it at Mac. He barked and jumped around, snapping at the jets of water. Sam tried to grab him to keep him still.

"Hey!" Sam spluttered, getting a faceful of water. "Mac's the one who needs a bath, Amelia. Not me!"

But he was laughing, and Amelia laughed too as she struggled to control the hose, which was twisting and coiling with the force of the water coming out. Soon she too was drenched.

Sam squeezed out some dog

shampoo and rubbed it into Mac's coat to make a soapy lather. Then Amelia hosed Mac down all over again. In a few moments Mac was dripping wet again, his fur plastered to his sides so that he looked half his normal size.

"We need a photo of this," Sam giggled, and ran inside to fetch his mum's phone. Amelia took it from him, pushing her dripping hair out of her eyes, opened the camera app and aimed at Sam and Mac. Just as she was taking the photo, Mac shook himself, spraying Amelia and Sam with water.

"Awesome!" said Sam when Amelia showed him the photo. His mouth was

wide open in a shout of laughter, and
Mac's mouth was open as if he was
laughing too. Sam's arms were around
the puppy, water droplets flying from
Mac's coat. "Maybe one day you could
be a wildlife photographer just like
Josh's mum."

Amelia suddenly had a brilliant idea.
She almost dropped the phone in her

excitement. "That's it!" she exclaimed. "Josh's mum – she must know everything about tracking animals. She can help us find the fox's mate!"

CHAPTER FIVE

Amelia sat impatiently on the sofa with her feet tucked underneath her. It was the next evening, and she was wearing warm clothes and her favourite green cap, which she had picked so she could blend in with the woods. When the bell rang, she jumped up and opened the door. Standing in the brisk evening air were Sam, Josh and Jenny Cleary, Josh's mum. They were wearing warm coats too.

"Let's go!" said Sam, hopping from foot to foot with excitement.

"Don't catch cold," advised Amelia's mum.

"Catch a fox instead!" added her gran. She pointed to the camera hanging around Josh's neck. "Or rather, catch one on camera."

In a few minutes, Amelia and the others were in the woods. The path was hard to see in the gathering dark. Josh's mum led the way with a torch in her hand and her night-vision camera around her neck. Her long red hair looked almost black in the dim light.

"Remember to keep together," she advised as they moved deeper among the trees. "And be as quiet as you can, so we don't disturb the animals."

Whenever there was a break in the tree cover, light from the full moon cast silver stripes across the leaves and undergrowth. *The wood is so different at night,* Amelia thought, the familiar path seeming like something strange and mysterious under her feet. Little creatures rustled in the undergrowth, and moths fluttered around the torch.

An owl hooted nearby and, somewhere in the distance, toads were croaking mournfully.

"This is amazing!" she whispered to Sam.

"I guess," he said, his voice a bit shaky. There was another owl hoot right

above their heads, and Sam stifled a yelp. "What was that?"

"Tawny owl," Josh's mum whispered. "Nothing to worry about."

"Thank goodness!" said Sam, his big eyes open wide.

Amelia giggled. "We'll keep you safe, Sam!" she whispered.

The path grew narrower as they approached the heart of the wood. There weren't many breaks in the trees now, and everything was very dark. Amelia's skin prickled as something brushed her leg, making her jump. *Just a leaf*, she told herself. *That's all*. She was starting to feel as nervous as Sam.

I hope we find the fox's mate soon!

There was a soft fluttering in the air. Dark shapes whooshed out from the trees, skimming above them like velvet darts. *Bats!* Amelia knew they were harmless creatures, but they looked very creepy flying out of the darkness. One swooped so close that it grazed her hair, making her duck.

"Get them off me!" Sam squeaked.

He darted off the path, his arms and hands flapping, vanishing from sight.

"Sam, wait!" Amelia ran after him, trying not to trip on the brambles she knew were lurking in the shadows. She could hardly see in the gloom. She didn't want to frighten away the animals – especially if the fox's mate was nearby – so she called as loudly as she dared. "Sam! Sam, come back!"

He was still crashing away from her. Amelia felt a pang of anxiety – they were getting further away from the others. She sped up. Her cap flew off and fell on the ground but she didn't stop to get it.

"Sam, we're supposed to stay on the path! Where are you?"

She bumped her arm painfully against a tree that loomed unexpectedly before her, its branches like long, snatching fingers. "*Sam!*"

Then she saw him. He had stopped running, and stood in a small moonlit clearing. He gave a wobbly laugh of relief when he saw her.

"The bats freaked me out," he said. "I just ran without thinking. Sorry."

"That's OK," said Amelia, "but we'd better stick together from now on. Come on, let's get back to Josh and his mum."

She looked around the clearing. Which direction had they come from? The path seemed to have vanished into the darkness. Amelia blundered around the clearing, Sam trailing after her. A cold, heavy dread settled in her stomach. They'd not only lost Josh and his mum, they'd lost the path as well. They were all alone in the dark woods.

"This is terrible," Sam moaned. "We're going to be stuck here for ever."

Amelia gritted her teeth. It was difficult not to panic. "We're going to be fine," she said, as bravely as she could.

"Can we sh–shout for help?" said Sam through chattering teeth.

Amelia tried to calm her racing heart. "If we shout, we'll scare off the animals. We'll have ruined the search."

Sam groaned. "I wish Mac was here."

So do I … Of course!

"Sam," Amelia gasped. "You know when Mac found the fox droppings?"

"Y-y-yes … ?"

"He was following a trail. We must have left a trail of our own when we ran through the woods just now." She glanced around their feet. "Come on, look for a place where the undergrowth is squashed down."

They hunted around the clearing, peering through the moon's faint

light for trampled ground.
Amelia was looking down
so carefully that she almost
walked right into a large tree that had
branches like fingers reaching out to
grab her …

"It's this way!" she said in excitement.
"I remember this tree!"

Amelia led the way, picking through
the bent fronds and branches and the
broken twigs underfoot. Suddenly, she
spotted something on the
ground. Bending
down, she picked up
the object, brushing
off the dirt.

"My cap!" she exclaimed, feeling a rush of relief. "We're definitely going the right way."

"Look over there!" Sam said.

A wavering torch beam illuminated the trees ahead. Amelia fought the urge to break into a run. She'd never been so pleased to see a torch in her life. She hurried through the trees towards it,

Sam following close behind her.

"Thank goodness!" said Josh's mum.
"I was about to start calling for you.
We thought you'd got lost."

"We did," Amelia confessed, panting a
little. "Any sign of the den?"

"Not yet," said Josh, shaking his head.
"Let's keep looking."

They carried on walking. Soon

they were in a part of the wood that Amelia hadn't seen before, far wilder than the place where she and Sam had met Dr Kent. The path was narrower here, with trees that pressed in on both sides. The leaves rustled like hundreds of whispering voices. And up ahead, they heard a strange, screaming cry – something between a cat's mew and a dog's bark.

Sam yelped. Amelia gasped. "What's that?" she asked, her heart racing. She'd never heard anything like it.

But Josh's mum was smiling at them. "That," she whispered, "is a fox!"

CHAPTER SIX

Amelia, Sam, Josh and Josh's mum crept towards the fox's eerie cry. They could hear cars beyond the trees, and Amelia realised that they were close to a main road – they had walked right through to the other side of the woods. The fox barked again, closer than before.

"I think she's calling for her mate," Josh whispered.

Amelia's heart clenched. It was certainly a lonely cry.

As they moved into a small clearing edged with beech trees, Josh's mum put her finger to her lips. Amelia peered through the darkness. At the other side of the clearing was a grassy mound among some brambles. And right in front of the mound sat a pale orange fox with a slim muzzle and pricked golden ears. Amelia clapped her hands to her mouth to stop herself from gasping out loud.

"So cool," murmured Sam beside her.

The fox tilted back her head and called again. Josh pressed the night-vision camera into Amelia's hand and silently showed her which buttons to press and how to zoom the lens. Amelia lifted it to her eye. It was heavier than a phone, and harder to hold steady, but every detail of the fox sprang into sharp focus. Amelia could see the dark patches on her muzzle, every hair on her ears, and the tip of her magnificent tail.

"She's so beautiful," Amelia breathed.

There was a sudden movement behind the fox. Four sets of ears came out of a hole in the mound, followed by four noses and four pairs of bright, glinting eyes. The fox had cubs! *And this must be their den*, Amelia realised.

The fox cubs' fur was fluffier than their mother's, and their ears seemed too large for their little bodies. Amelia grinned as the cubs tumbled over each other, chasing and pouncing and biting each other's tails. They reminded her of Caramel's kittens.

Amelia passed the camera around. Josh's mouth fell open when he saw

the cubs, Josh's mum gave a gasp, and
Sam grinned in delight. Then his eyes
went wide. He passed the camera back
to Amelia. "Look what they're playing
with!" he whispered.

Amelia adjusted the zoom. It was
hard to make anything out at first.
Then Amelia saw five black fingers …
The cubs were playing with one of Mr
Ferguson's motorbike gloves! The other

glove flopped sadly beside the mouth of the den, chewed to pieces.

"I knew it wasn't Mac!" whispered Sam. "We're actually really close to the B&B here, so it makes sense."

"They must have somehow got the gloves off your parents' washing line," Amelia whispered back. She took a picture. "Now we've got proof! Even Mr Ferguson will have to believe you now."

Josh's mum took several more pictures of the den and the surrounding area. "They'll help us find the den again," she explained. "Now, we'd better go. We don't want to disturb them."

They crept back out of the clearing.

As she went, Amelia gave the fox family one last glance over her shoulder. The cubs were lying quietly now, sprawled on the forest floor. Still as a statue, the mother fox sat and watched over them. All was quiet in the woods – except for the roar of a car passing by on the main road.

This isn't a safe home for them, Amelia thought. She hated the idea of another member of the fox family being hit by a car. *There must be something we can do to help …*

CHAPTER SEVEN

Mrs Hope looked a little startled to
see Amelia, Sam and Josh at the door
of the surgery as soon as it opened on
Monday morning.

"Is something wrong?" she asked the
children. "Have you found another
injured animal?"

"No, nothing like that," said Amelia. "We just wondered if we could visit the fox before we go to school."

"Is he OK?" Josh asked.

"He's doing very well," said Mrs Hope, ushering them inside the surgery. "We've got him in a pen away from the other animals so he's got peace and quiet. You have to remember, he's not used to being around people – or dogs and cats."

She showed them to the little window set into a consulting-room door.

"There he is," she said. "Safe and sound, and getting better all the time. Don't go inside, though. The less contact he has with people, the better."

Amelia, Sam and Josh pressed their faces to the little window. The fox was moving around more easily than the last time they had seen him, but he seemed restless as he prowled back and forth, stopping occasionally to eat some food from a bowl.

"We think he's ready to go back into the wild," said Mr Hope, who had come to join them. "Now all we need to do is find his den."

Amelia, Sam and Josh all grinned at each other.

"Well," said Amelia. "We've managed to do that. We found it last night."

"You did?" cried Mrs Hope. "That's wonderful!"

Amelia felt a rush of pride at how pleased the two vets looked. "Josh, could you show Mr and Mrs Hope the pictures?"

The vets studied the images on Josh's camera. "It looks like a good spot," said

Mr Hope. "Plenty of cover, and an open area for the cubs to play in. Where is it?"

"That's the thing," said Josh. "You can't see it in the pictures, but there's another road really close by."

"We're worried that one of the foxes will be hit by a car again," Amelia said. She'd woken up very early that morning, too anxious about the foxes to go back to sleep.

Mr Hope nodded gravely. "That is a concern," he said. "Perhaps we should try to relocate the whole family."

Mrs Hope's forehead furrowed. "They would need somewhere sheltered. Far from the road, and not too near people either. But I can't think of anywhere like that."

A memory stirred in Amelia's mind. She'd seen somewhere like that recently, she was sure of it. But where? *Come on, I need to remember!*

"Let's all give it some thought," said Mr Hope. "Now, isn't it time you went off to school?"

Amelia was still racking her brains as they walked back into the waiting room. She could picture dark holes, dug deep into the ground somewhere in the woods. Holes big enough for …

"Badgers!" she cried.

The Hopes looked startled.

"Badgers?" said Josh with a puzzled frown.

The memory rushed through Amelia now, as clear as day. "Sam and I passed an abandoned badger sett yesterday, in the woodland near the B&B. Could we move the fox family there?"

Mr and Mrs Hope looked at each other thoughtfully.

"Foxes do sometimes live in old setts," said Mrs Hope, nodding. "It's quite sensible, really. Why go to the trouble of digging yourself a hole when someone else has already done all the hard work for you?"

Mr Hope's eyes gleamed. "It's certainly

worth a try," he agreed. "Do you think you could find it again?"

Sam nodded. "Definitely."

"Great!" said Mrs Hope. "Our friend Nick runs a wildlife centre a few miles from here. We'll see if he can help."

"Can we help too?" asked Amelia hopefully.

Mrs Hope laughed. "Something tells me we won't be able to stop you!"

CHAPTER EIGHT

"This is amazing!" gasped Amelia. They
stood beside a hide Josh's mum had
built close to the abandoned badger sett.
Amelia's mum and Gran had come to
see it too. Amelia ran her hand over the
sturdy wood panels, the early-morning
light playing across its green paint and

the camouflage netting draped over it. There was a slot – like the one in a postbox, but bigger – for whoever was inside the hide to look out of.

"Thank you, Amelia," said Ms Cleary with a smile. She checked her phone. "Right! Mrs Hope says the foxes are on their way. Time to get into the hide!"

They all squeezed in. The hide had a step in front of the window slot, and Amelia, Sam and Josh stood on it so they could see out, while Josh's mum, Amelia's mum and Gran stood behind them. They were all very quiet.

It wasn't long before Amelia heard footsteps crunching through the

undergrowth. Peering through the slot,
she saw three figures emerge through
the trees, each carrying a large metal
box. Mr and Mrs Hope were bundled up
against the morning chill in snug fleeces
and hats. The other man, who Amelia
realised must be their friend Nick from

the wildlife centre, had a brown and grey beard that reminded her of a badger. They all put their boxes down gently in front of the sett.

Sam nudged Amelia. "Here we go!" he whispered.

At a nod from Nick, the Hopes opened the doors of their boxes. Then Nick opened the door of his own box, and the three adults hurried to join them in the hide.

"Now we have to cross our fingers that this works," Nick whispered.

A long snout poked out of one of the boxes. Amelia held her breath

as the male fox emerged. His pointed
ears were pricked, and he sniffed the
dawn air. His leg and ear were both
completely healed now, and he moved
easily as he snuffled at the other boxes.
He must be so pleased to be outside again,
Amelia thought.

The female fox stepped out of her
box, peering around curiously. Then she
stared at the male fox. He stared back.

"Let's hope they remember each
other," murmured Mrs Hope.

The pair padded towards each other.
Then their noses touched, and Amelia
felt a swell of joy as the male fox
rubbed his head against the vixen's

side. The cubs came out of their box, tumbling over each other. The largest cub scampered to the old badger sett and sniffed at it – then trotted into one of the holes.

Please let them all like their new home, Amelia thought.

The mother fox followed her cub inside. The other cubs went after her. Finally, the male fox went inside. Amelia glanced around the hide. Everyone was smiling with relief and happiness.

The fox family darted in and out of the sett, the cubs playing together, rolling and squirming in the undergrowth while their parents looked on. Watching them, Amelia wanted to help at Animal Ark more than ever – watching these wild animals was so special. Beside her, Josh raised his camera and began taking photos.

"Wow," he whispered, snapping away at the family of foxes.

"Can I see?" asked Amelia.

Josh shook his head, grinning. "You'll have to wait. I've just taken the photo I'm going to enter into the competition!"

It had been several days since they released the foxes, and Amelia and Sam had spent most of their free time teaching Mac not to pull on his lead. Whenever he pulled too hard, they turned around and took him home – no matter how much Mac whined, or stared pleadingly up at them. Now it was the

evening of the photography competition,
and Amelia, Sam and their families were
on their way to Animal Ark, looking
forward to seeing the entries. Amelia's
mum and gran were chatting to Sam's
parents, while Mac trotted between Sam
and Amelia.

"He's being so good," said Sam
proudly. "He's not pulling on
his lead at all."

Amelia leaned
down to pat Mac's
furry head. "I
knew we'd be able
to train him," she
said. "Well done, Mac."

"And if he keeps getting better," said Sam, "Mum and Dad will have to let me keep him!"

When they reached Animal Ark, there was already a large crowd in the waiting room, where the competition entries were on display. Julia and Simon, the veterinary nurse, were handing out refreshments, and the room was loud with laughter and conversation. Amelia recognised several people, including her teacher Miss Hafiz, in a glittering purple headscarf, and Dr Kent, who wore a smart suit. Nick from the wildlife centre waved from across the room.

The walls were hung with photos, all

blown up to poster-size. Some were in colour, others were black and white. There were photos of dogs, cats, chickens and even a bearded lizard, which was sitting on a rock and displaying its spiny throat.

Josh was standing with his mum beside his photograph. Amelia gasped as she took it in. It showed two of the fox cubs standing on their hind legs, lit by the first golden rays of the morning sun as they playfully grappled with each other. In the background, inside one of the badger sett's tunnels, were several glowing pairs of fox eyes. Amelia and Sam went over to join Josh and his mum.

"Your photo is incredible!" Amelia told Josh.

"Amazing," said Sam.

"Thanks!" Josh's cheeks turned pink. "I like your picture too."

"Oh, yes," said Sam, "there it is!"

The photo Amelia had taken of Sam

and Mac was hanging beside Josh's entry. Both Sam and Mac seemed to be laughing at the camera, drops of water flying around them.

"Mac's famous!" Amelia said with a laugh. "And so are you, Sam!"

"Ahem," said a deep voice.

Amelia and Sam turned around. Mr Ferguson was standing before them.

"I, er … seem to owe Mac an apology," said Mr Ferguson. He scratched at his beard as if he were uncomfortable. "Your parents showed me the photo of the foxes with my gloves. I'm sorry that I blamed your puppy, Sam. It just … Well, it did seem as if …"

"That's all right," said Sam.

"Good." Mr Ferguson bent down and gave Mac an awkward pat. Mac barked and licked his hand.

"Did you enter the competition?" Amelia asked.

A blush stole up from beneath Mr

Ferguson's beard and crept over his cheeks. "I did, as a matter of fact," he said. "That one's mine, over there."

He gestured at a photo of three fluffy ducklings paddling across the village pond. Amelia bit her lip, trying not to smile. *I don't think Mr Ferguson is as mean as he wants everyone to think!*

There was the squeal of a microphone, and the room fell silent.

"Welcome, everyone, to the Animal Ark photo competition," said Mrs Hope. She was standing in the centre of the reception room, holding a mic. "We are so delighted with all the fantastic photos you see hanging here today. It was very hard for us to choose the winners. First up is the prize for the Funniest Photo. And that goes to … Amelia Haywood and Sam Baxter!"

Amelia and Sam whooped. Sam cuddled Mac proudly as Amelia went up to collect their prize from Mr Hope – a dog-grooming kit for Mac.

The bearded lizard photo won the Most Unusual Animal prize, and Mr Ferguson beamed at the applause for his ducklings, which won the Cutest Photo award.

"And finally," said Mrs Hope, "the grand prize of Best Photo. All the photos here are brilliant, but our overall winner is very special indeed. I'm delighted to announce that the winner is … Josh Cleary!"

Josh flushed as red as his hair as the room burst into applause.

Amelia cheered as he collected his prize money from Mrs Hope, while Mr Hope stuck a rosette next to the photograph.

"What are you going to spend your prize on, Josh?" Sam asked. "A new camera?"

Josh shook his head. "I've thought of something even better." He turned to Mr and Mrs Hope. "Would it be all right if I showed Caramel and her kittens to Mum?"

"Of course you can," Mr Hope said. "Amelia and Sam, why don't you take them through?"

Amelia and Sam led Josh and his mum through the door into the room at the back of the surgery. In her pen, Caramel blinked when she saw them, and rolled lazily on to her side. The four kittens put their paws up against the bars as Amelia carefully unlatched the cage.

"Oh, they're adorable!" Josh's mum exclaimed.

Josh reached in and picked up the ginger kitten. It started purring immediately, nuzzling its whiskers into his hand.

"Mum says I can adopt him," he said, stroking the kitten's tiny head.

"Really?" cried Amelia. "That's brilliant!"

"I liked this little guy right away," Josh explained. "He reminds me of the foxes. And he was the only one who wasn't scared of my camera! So I'm going to spend my prize money on the things I'll need to look after him, like a basket and some toys."

"Cool!" said Sam. "What are you going to call him?"

Josh smiled. "Flash, of course!"

What a perfect week, Amelia thought happily, as she and Sam petted Caramel and the tortoiseshell kittens, while Josh and his mum fussed over Flash. They had rescued an injured fox, rehomed his family, and found another kitten a home. Now there was just one more kitten to go.

We promised Mr and Mrs Hope we would find homes for all the kittens, and I think we're going to do it, she thought. *And then maybe they'll let me and Sam help out here all the time …*

What adventures would she have next at Animal Ark? Something told her she wouldn't have to wait long to find out!

The End

Turn the page for a sneak peek at
Amelia and Sam's next adventure!

ANIMAL ARK

Puppy in Peril

Lucy Daniels

Julia called out, "Good news!"

Amelia's heart lifted. "You've found the puppy's owner?"

The receptionist's face fell. "Not that, I'm afraid. We've found a sanctuary who can take the last kitten. They'll be coming to pick her up next week."

"Oh," said Amelia, trying to sound cheerful. "That's … great news."

They left Mac with Julia, who dried his fur with a towel.

The puppy found near the motorway was in a pen, her head resting on her paws. Her ears were drooping.

"Is she any better?" Amelia asked Mrs Hope, who was checking the poorly puppy's breathing with her stethoscope.

"We confirmed that she needs an operation," said Mrs Hope. "She's still very ill."

"And no sign of the owner?" said Sam.

Mrs Hope shook her head. "I've just given the puppy a painkiller. That should make her more comfortable. Would you like to say hello? I'm sure she'd like to see some friendly faces."

Amelia stroked the puppy's head gently. She wagged her tail weakly. *If she does have an owner somewhere, she must be missing her terribly*, thought Amelia.

"Don't worry. We're going to help you," she said. "I promise."

The next morning, Sam and Mac arrived at Amelia's after breakfast. It was still raining, and they were both soaked through.

"Any news?" Sam asked, as they went upstairs.

Amelia shook her head. Her mum had let her phone Animal Ark first thing that morning to find out if the puppy's owner had come forward. But no one had got in touch.

Amelia felt as if she had a big weight in her tummy. The posters, the flyers … What if was all for nothing? She flopped on to the window seat in her bedroom. Sam slumped beside her and

Mac lay at their feet.

"What are we going to do?" asked Sam with a groan. "If she was found by the motorway, the owner might not even live around here. They might never see our posters."

Amelia realised he was right. They sat for a long time, thinking about what to do. With every day that passed the puppy's condition would get worse.

"We've got to save her," said Amelia. "So if we can't find the owner ... we'll just have to pay for the operation ourselves!"

"But how?" asked Sam. "I haven't got two thousand pounds, and I'm guessing you haven't either."

Amelia twirled a lock of hair between her fingers, thinking hard. Suddenly, she remembered the conversation with the TV crew.

"You know what Mr Ferguson said yesterday? About motorbike shows?"

Sam nodded. "You should have seen him this morning," he said. "He wanted to show the film crew his motorbike. He kept going outside to see if they were around, but they weren't filming because of the rain. He *really* wants to be on telly. I saw him looking at himself out on the hall mirror, wearing his helmet and his leathers."

Amelia laughed. "What if we organised a show of our own?" she said. "That way we might be able to get enough money!"

"A motorbike show?" Sam asked, looking confused.

"No, a dog show!" said Amelia. "We could charge for entry."

A grin spread across Sam's lips. "Brilliant idea!"

Two hours later, their friends Izzy and Josh were sitting in Amelia's bedroom. The floor was covered with pieces of paper they'd scribbled over, and there were half-drunk mugs of hot chocolate by their sides. It was still pouring outside, with rain lashing the window, but the room was full of bright excitement.

"What have we got so far?" asked Josh.

Amelia read from her notebook, which was covered in animal stickers. "Date and time: Saturday at 10am. Location: Mr Stevens's barn."

"It was really nice of him to say we could have the show there," said Sam.

"My mum has got planks and poles to make the agility course," Izzy said. "And Mr Stevens has other stuff we can use for the events."

"My mum and Gran will collect the money at the door," said Amelia.

"Where's the list of events?" asked Josh.

Sam scooped up Mac and took the piece of paper he was sitting on. "Here it is! We've got Best Trick, Best Groomed Dog, Dog Most Like Its Owner, Best Paw Shaker, Waggiest Tail, Most Obedient and an Obstacle Course."

"This is going to be so much fun," said Amelia. "Now we just need some contestants. We have to spread the word!"

"I can do that," said Josh.

"Me too!" said Izzy.

"And Sam and I can go to Animal Ark to ask the Hopes if they could be the judges," said Amelia. "Let's go!"

Read **Puppy in Peril** to find out what happens next …

Animal Advice

Do you love animals as much as Amelia and Sam? Here are some tips on how to look after them from veterinary surgeon Sarah McGurk.

Caring for your pet

1. Animals need clean water at all times.
2. They need to be fed too – ask your vet what kind of food is best, and how much the animal needs.
3. Some animals, such as dogs, need exercise every day
4. Animals also need lots of love. You should always be very gentle with your pets and be careful not to do anything that might hurt them.

When to go to the vet

Sometimes animals get ill. Like you, they will mostly get better on their own. But if your pet has hurt itself or seems very unwell, then a trip to the vet might be needed. Some pets also need to be vaccinated, to prevent them from getting dangerous diseases. Your vet can tell you what your pet needs.

Helping wildlife

- Always ask an adult before you go near any animals you don't know.
- If you find an animal or bird which is injured or can't move, it is best not to touch it.
- If you are worried, you can phone an animal charity such as the RSPCA (SSPCA in Scotland) for help.

ANIMAL ARK

Where animals need you!

COLLECT ALL OF AMELIA AND SAM'S EXCITING ADVENTURES!

Kitten Rescue
Lucy Daniels

Bunny Trouble
Lucy Daniels

Fox Cub Danger
Lucy Daniels

Puppy in Peril
Lucy Daniels

www.animalark.co.uk

🐾 Discover all the books in the series
🐾 Read exciting extracts
🐾 Find fun downloads
🐾 And lots more!